HE IS ROYAL

LEBOHANG ANGELINAH MOKHELE

Published by

Macher Afrika Publishers

Printed and bound in Durban,
South Africa

ISBN: 978-0-620-87615-5

Acknowledgements

To my family, mom, and the boys; Dite and Thato, thank you so much for putting up with my mood swings when I'm glued to my laptop and dodging all house chores. You guys are my pillars of strength.

My sisters, especially Portia, Bangi, and Ithabeleng thank you for not suing me, I've probably violated you in many ways than one. My extended family, thank you so much.

My father and mentor Prophet Ernest Mahlaba, I thank God for manifesting true love through you. You've believed in me even when I doubted myself, for that I'm grateful. This is your product!

To all my friends and former classmates from Seforong Primary, St. Mary's and Tsakholo High School as well as The National University of Lesotho, thank you for colouring my life with memories, you continue to inspire me.

To my family at Communion Bible Ministries, thank you for your prayers.

To my Golden Team, thank you for showing me the system that has made my dream a reality.

My publisher and dear friend, Nompumelelo Gcaba, thank you for being my midwife in delivering this baby.

Most importantly, I will extend my gratitude to you Reader for the effort to travel with me, happy reading!

Special thanks to Dumisane Radebe and Dikeledi Motaung (cover models) as well as everyone who contributed towards the success of Mohlanka Wa Modimo short film.

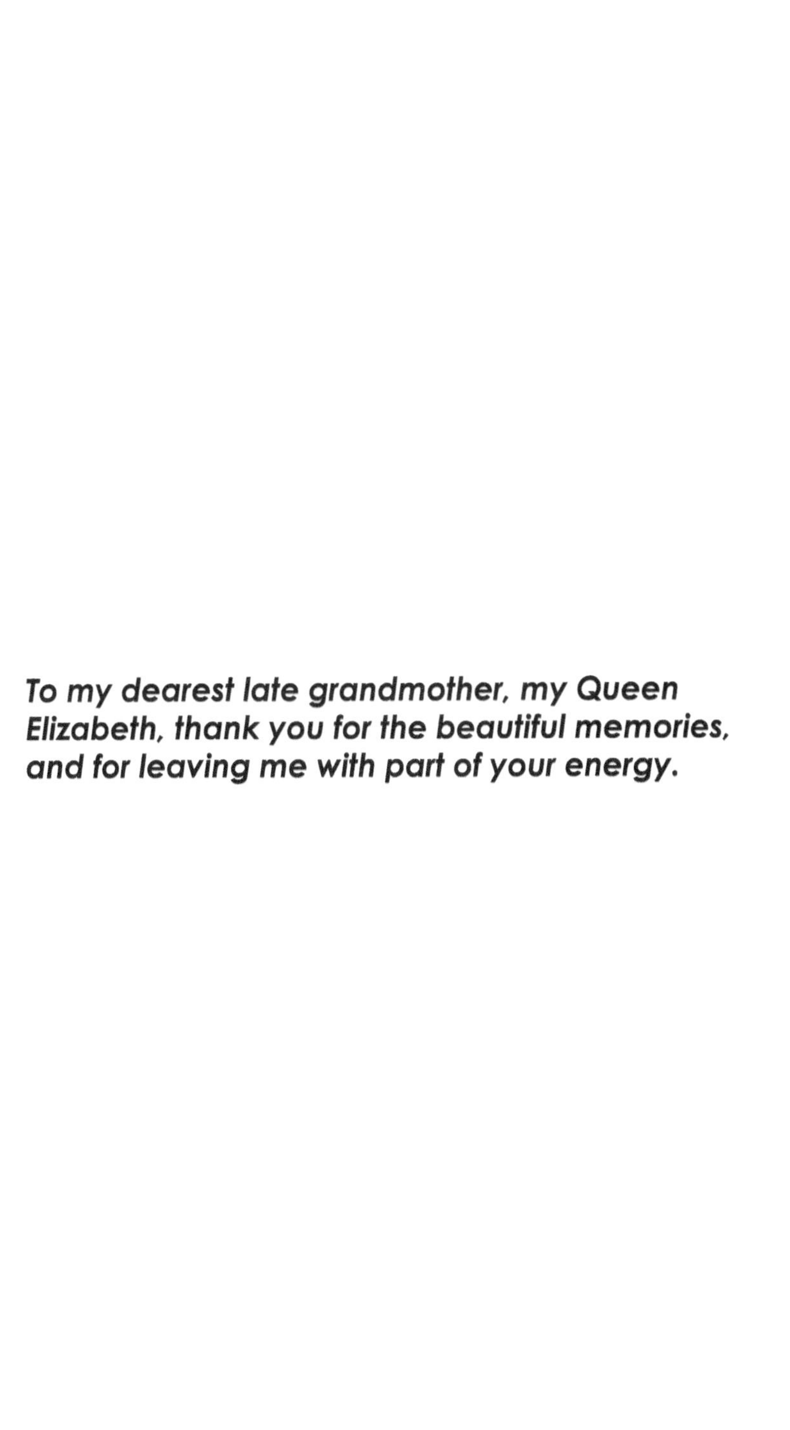

To my dearest late grandmother, my Queen Elizabeth, thank you for the beautiful memories, and for leaving me with part of your energy.

1.

"Yes, *ausi* Kate. I hear you loud and clear. I will make a plan soon." Bangani said lightly, exhaling a deflated sigh and rolling her eyes, conscious that her caller cannot see her.

"You better, *my kind!* This is the only condition for you to access the inheritance. Trust your father to be demanding even from beneath the ground. I don't understand why he had to add such a byzantine clause." Kate sounded a little worried, wondering how Bangani took their conversation lightly in spite of its ghastly demands.

"Will you please relax? I've got this." Bangani assured confidently. "I've got to go now, I love you."

"Ek is lief vir jou, my kind!"

Bangani Khumalo, an adorable naturally warm looking woman in her mid-twenties was speaking to her mother, whom she calls sister because she grew up at her grandmother's with cousins and extended siblings who called her mother *ausi* Kate. Kate left Bangani, at the tender age of 6 months, in her mother's care when she got offered a job in Cape Town. It was not long after she had turned down Zachariah's proposal to leave South Africa to Amsterdam where he was offered a delegate position.

Kate and Zachariah, or Zac as Kate affectionately called him, had a lot in common -specially their love for the finer things in life, hence Zac's devastation when she rejected his offer. He had assumed that eloping to the Netherlands would be warmly accepted by his lover and baby mama.

Unfortunately for Zac, Kate had her valid reasons for declining the crème de la crème lifestyle. She was a new mother. She needed the guidance of her much more experienced mother, Zandile, in her new journey. She felt she could not cope with motherhood in a foreign country with Zac busy acclimatising himself in a new and higher position. She had even suffered post-natal depression when infant Bangani thought she was 'too cool' for breastmilk. The two parents grew apart as both embarked on their arduous missions. Although Zac ensured that mother and baby were financially catered for, Kate wanted her own money. She wanted to fulfil her dream to leave Clarens on her own accord and look for greener pastures, or rather, blue waters.

When she left Bangani at such a critical stage of infancy, Zac was infuriated by her decision. Particularly after she rejected taking the leap of faith with him. Stubborn Kate felt no pang of guilt and even provoked Zac to come fetch his child if he felt he could do a better job at parenting. The scuffle grew them further apart until Zac stopped calling altogether. Duty-bound to his daughter, he would send gifts and money as often as possible.

Bangani knew that she would see her mother once a year, during Christmas. And she had no problem with this long distance relationship as she received enough attention from her grandmother. Amongst the rest of the family, she was the apple of her grandmother's eye. She highly esteemed her absent father from a distance for most of her childhood until her teens when she became techno-smart and she started communicating with him via Skype.

The two became incredibly close although they were worlds apart. Zac even invited Bangani to visit him and his family in Amsterdam. After that, they took turns on hosting these vacations yearly, although often, he opted that they met in Cape Town. He had a luxurious penthouse not far from Kate's bachelor flat. Of course Bangani had no problem with it as she loved seeing both her parents. On the other hand, Kate hated these chance meetings with her ex-lover who was still head over heels in love with her. But then again, their luck had run out as Zac was then a married man with twin boys whom Bangani adored dearly.

After matric, Bangani left Clarens and went to study Art Curation at a college in Cape Town. Zac offered her his apartment but she chose to live with her mother. Mother and daughter bonded after the passing of Mani Zandi a few months later. Kate took the motherhood role on fully, even though Bangani stuck to calling her *ausi* Kate and occasionally mother, but never mom.

Kate was stunned when one day she found her daughter packing her belongings in a luggage for travel. When she asked, she was flatly told that Bangani was going back to the Free State, for good.

"*Liefie, maar hoekom?* I thought we were getting along just fine. Did I do something wrong?" Kate groused still in shock by the sudden decision that Bangani had taken.

"No, *ausi* Kate. It's not about you. This is a personal quest that I must take if ever I want to create something meaningful with my life."

"What do you mean meaningful, *my kind*? You have a good life here with me, and you love your job which you excel at. There are plenty of guys asking you out which you constantly turn down, only God knows why!"

"I don't mean to be ungrateful, mother. I just feel like there's treasure that needs to be discovered in Clarens. Plus, here I feel quite detached from Mani Zandi's spirit." She wore a stern look and when Kate matched her gaze, she noticed something in her daughter that she had not seen before. Her sincerity when she spoke about her granny was unmatched, and Kate knew from that look that she was fighting a losing battle where her own mother was concerned.

"Okay, *liefie*. I know that you don't need my approval, but please hear me, I'll give you my blessing on one condition."

"Name it."

"You will come home for Christmas."

"Sorry, *ausi* Kate. You and dad owe me a Christmas back home and I'll be more than delighted to host this year."

"Oh dear, I certainly do not see why not; *maar*, good luck convincing Zac to go to the Free State."

"Well, it's non-negotiable. I've already sent Mildred the pictures of the aesthetic Golden Gate mountains and she took the bait. She's my bargaining chip if dad dares to come up with an excuse."

"I didn't know that she was also invited, but if it's the only way to get your dad to his abandoned hometown, then who am I to object?"

"Yep, she is my only hope. Plus, I owe Nate and Niel lots of adventure. What are big sisters for?"

"Now that you say it, it could be fun to have a big family Christmas in memory of Mani Zandi."

"Thank you, dear mother. I knew that you'd come to the party. Does it mean that I have your blessings?" She inquired teasingly, spreading her arms to receive some tender loving care.

"*Kom hier, liefie.* You are already blessed, *my kind.*" She hugged and kissed her fondly.

Driving a stoutly loaded black and lime Jeep Sahara into a mini town of Clarens surrounded by high mountains, brought a smile of satisfaction to a determined Bangani. She slid down the windows to fully inhale the afternoon autumn breeze that was starting to feel a bit chilly for April. She came to a halt in front of her favourite traditional pizza house, Vito's, where she had a meet and greet with her cousin and best friend, Ithabeleng. After their meal which Bangani kept raving about the entire drive, they both went to Mani Zandi's to see the rest of the family.

Bangani's last stop was next to a neglected former bridal shop which closed down because the owner left for New York. She fell in love with the place right away as it revived so many memories; how she used to stop by every Saturday afternoon with Mani Zandi to admire flower girl gowns that she would wear to a nativity play at church. She recalled how she used to try-on the oversized pearls and fascinators and pose in front of the mirror while Mani Zandi would watch her dotingly without getting bored by this monotonous performance.

Later on, Mani Zandi would reveal a surprise gift of a pair of knee-high white lacy socks and Bangani would be so elated that her grandmother had taken a hint while she subtly browsed her fingers through them without fussing or making a blatant request. The sight of her favourite spot on the first day of her arrival in Clarens brought what she missed while in Cape Town. She had never felt so intimate with her grandmother in her absentia and she knew right away that she had made the right call.

Bangani was reminiscing about how it all began, the shop that now seemed to be her entire life, the one that she chose; the one that brought fulfilment and reason to wake up daily. She then realised how it had taken so much of her that she had not even bothered to entertain any guys asking her out. In her defence, she was too busy building a monumental empire that brought her the utmost contentment that she felt there was no need to settle down with anyone until... *well until Lord Zachariah demanded.*

Although she was able to convince her mother that she had a plan on how to fully access her late father's inheritance, it only dawned to her that she actually had no idea where to begin. All she knew and was determined to do was to get her naturally manicured hands on her Birthright at all costs. She could already see a substantial injection that money would do to her business. The expansion and mass market penetration, the works. In her mind, she witnessed being South Africa's best curator and art collector.

Because she had long defaulted on the social calendar of events with her friends, she knew that only Ithabeleng would know what was happening over the weekend and even hook her up with the next available hottest date. That would be the first step, nevertheless, surviving a blind date was the least of her worries, she had to find the perfect man to marry her.

He must be from the royal family.

Zac's deep voice resonated in her mind. She could even depict the stern look that he wore while dictating these terms to his lawyer.

You are a difficult man Zachariah Khumalo! She murmured under her breath while smiling at an approaching client.

Letlotlo, a fine looking and well-built young man almost the same age as Bangani, came to the counter with two bundles of wooden key holders engraved **JESUS IS KING** and placed them in front of Bangani, beaming with consummation. "*Wa bona* BK, this is a great design, and the glossy finish is absolutely superb."

He pronounced, admiringly tracing his forefinger on the engraved message.

"I'm glad you loved them, else I would have lost my favourite client." Bangani smiled at him taking one key holder from his hand, their fingers touched and they both felt the inferno as their gazes met.

Get your grip, Bangani. She did not. Instead she stared teasingly at him to search if he also felt that blaze or if her mind was merely playing tricks on her.

Letlotlo quickly broke the gaze and cleared his throat. "When is the next batch making it to the shelves?"

"It's also at the back. I assumed Roxanne would show you. I did not want to put it on display before you got your order sorted; you know I wouldn't have been able to keep them away from inquisitive clients."

"Smart move. I'm pretty sure that some of them would be the ones from church, that would have ruined my surprise altogether."

"You definitely owe me coffee then." Innocent as that sounded, she wished she could find a padlock to lock her loose mouth that seemed to do more good in betraying her that afternoon.

"Oh, don't you worry. It goes without saying. I do have another huge favour to ask you though, that's if I'm not pushing my luck."

"Yes! I will marry you." *Bangani! What is wrong with you?* She almost pinched herself in admonition.

"You will?" He could not hide his elation.

She giggled awkwardly. "I am kidding, Tlotla. Of course not."

A bit disappointed, he exhaled flatly and shrugged. "Oh well! Forgive a guy for counting his lucky stars prematurely."

"Serves you right, are you out of your mind?"

Letlotlo grimaced half-dotingly. "Come on. Would it be that bad to end up together, I've practically known you my entire life."

"That's what makes it even more awkward." She switched her focus. "What is the huge favour that you wanted to ask?"

"Would you be so kind as to keep these off the shelves at least until after the youth conference please? I wouldn't want anyone getting their hands on these before they're taught of the kingdom principles."

"*Hao*, Tlotla! How long have you been a regular? It goes without saying. It is just a few days away, right?"

"Yep, next weekend, you coming?"

For a second, his question sent a sensual heat to her plumpy cheeks. *Oh God, what is happening to me?*

"I thought you'd never ask. Of course I'd love to. I'll just have to make arrangements with Roxanne to help me lock up. Do count me in"

"It's a date then." He affirmed.

"I suppose it is." She agreed modestly.

Letlotlo couldn't hide his excitement as he was almost out of the shop and he wished he could linger on the spicy jasmine and cinnamon fragrance that Bangani wore as she neared to see him out. "I can hardly wait."

"*Ha-ha*! You will be strong. I'll see you then."

"Keep well!"

Both of them smiled awkwardly at this mutual agreement. Bangani had always known that Letlotlo was secretly fond of her and she disregarded the hints that Ithabeleng threw in that regard.

"The church boy is crushing on you bigtime, *mmata*. When are you indulging?" Ithabeleng would tease.

"*Mmata wena,* according to you I must indulge on every Tom, Dick and Harry. Even the ones that are clearly not my type." Bangani would dismiss her without entertaining the idea.

When she was convinced that Letlotlo was out of earshot, she quickly ran to her phone and speed dialled Ithabeleng.

"*Mmata*, how did you know I was about to call you?" Ithabeleng asked, almost out of her breath.

"Telepathy, darling! You go first. What's up?"

"Tele... what? You and your Cape Town English. It's okay *mmata, bua.*"

"Okay, I have exciting news. But promise me that you won't laugh." Bangani cleared, cautious not to expose herself to her bestie although she knew that she was as transparent as *consol*. Whenever she hid anything from Ithabeleng, there was no point as she always had her all figured out.

"Out with it already, you know I can't promise you that."

"I finally agreed to a date with Tlotla." Bangani bawled enthusiastically.

"Why am I not surprised? Poor church boy must have been at the right place at the right time." Ithabeleng responded a bit sardonically.

"Will you stop calling him that? Wait... she called you too, hasn't she? Why am I not surprised?"

"You know she means well. She wants only what's best for you."

"*Aa mmata, ausi* Kate thinks I'm incapable of finding my own date. Well, you can tell her, not this time"

"Okay, sweetheart, calm down. You know none of us think you're incapable. When are you going on a date?"

"Never mind, what did you want to say?" Bangani's mood dampened but Ithabeleng knew that it was to be expected.

"Come on, *mmata*. Don't be like that." She had to strike while the iron was still hot. "Anyway, drop whatever you have scheduled tonight. We've got karaoke at Andy's."

"*Mmata*, I love karaoke, but I will pass. Tonight I just want to have a quiet evening."

"Oh yeah, how insensitive of me? You do want to regurgitate Zac's Will. Say no more, I'll bring wine. And forget about the pots, I'll get mac and cheese too."

"Says the maid of honour at my façade wedding. On a mission to get me a husband and feeding me mac and cheese at the same time. You are dismally failing at a simple task, Ithabeleng Snyman."

They both laughed.

"Oh no, sweetheart. I'm far from failing. Wait until tonight. You have absolutely no idea what I've got up my sleeve."

"I can already imagine. Let me go assist Roxanne at the back. See you tonight."

"See you, *mamoruti!*" Ithabeleng said conventionally, giggling as she hung up before Bangani rebuked her.

Bangani knew that this was going to be a long night. And she needed all the energy she could get. She went to the posterior of her shop where her assistant was busy unpacking new stock and pricing.

***

Inside Clarens Kingdom Fellowship Church, Letlotlo was moving sturdily past the arrayed chairs, noting that the sound system was ready for the choir and eying the pulpit which was reverentially set aside not far from the passage that leads towards Pastor Jerry Makhethe's office. The door swirl opened before he could knock. Mama Jerry, a kind looking woman of about late forties came out with a tray of used fine porcelain tea set.

"Tlotla, you gave me quite a scare. Are you alright, *ngwana ka?*" she beamed.

"*Ke hantle*, mama. Is daddy busy? I've got to show him these." Letlotlo indicated the carrier pack that Bangani had skilfully wrapped his key holders in. His light cheeks suddenly became feverish at the thought of watching Bangani's hands and he wondered what else those hands could do. The mere imagination sent undeniable excitement to his cores.

Stop it Letlotlo! You're in a church for crying out loud.

"*Kena*, son. You know that your father doesn't mind your intrusion. I'll bring tea and scones."

"*Kea leboha,* mama. You'll see these shortly." He gave way to his mother who eyed the package nosily.

"Come on in already, son. Curiosity is getting the better of me here. *Mama, etsa o kgutle hle.*" Pastor Jerry interrupted and both Letlotlo and Mama Jerry shrugged and giggled as they separated.

"Afternoon, Daddy. I'm sorry I took a bit long, evangelising." Letlotlo chirped in almost breathlessly, shutting the door behind him.

"Son, you're in the house of God and you think you can lie to me?"

"*Hao!* Daddy, what could I possibly lie about?"

"So, trying to woo Bangani is regarded as evangelism now?" Pastor Jerry asked quizzically, wearing the *I-See-You* face.

"How we are always this translucent to you is both unfair and dangerous, daddy. My humble apologies." Letlotlo regretted lying to his father.

"I'm sorry too, son. I don't mean to invade your privacy. I can't help but put you under 24-hour surveillance. It's the only way to get my spirit to rest; knowing that you are not under any form of attack."

"It's alright, daddy. I know you mean well."

"I've let my guard down once, and it almost landed us in humiliation. Not again, son."

"I've learnt my lesson, trust me. Besides, this is different."

"She is a good one. I've noticed how you look at her."

"*Eish*, daddy. You have no idea, the mere sight of her makes my heart jump in leaps and bounds. If only it were that simple to tell her my intentions."

"Do you want me to intervene? We can influence the spiritual realm anytime you say the word, son. I know her grandmother would approve."

"Thank you, daddy. I think I will take this one as a personal mission. One day at a time. Speaking of Gogo Zandile, her remarkable character is what I see and love about BK. I know she hardly comes to the church, contrary to her granny, but my heart is fond of her."

"What are you waiting for then? Make your move! A girl like her must have a queue of hot-blooded men awaiting their turn to waltz and dine her."

"Oh! I've made it past that somewhat impenetrable list. Daddy will be proud to know that I finally asked her on a date, and she has agreed."

"It sure took a lot of will power. Nonetheless, I am happy for you, son."

"Thank you, daddy. She does make me nervous though. I literally become a noodle in hot soup."

They both chuckled.

Letlotlo loved how easy it was to speak to his parents about anything. They had an intimate and a spiritual relationship in which all parties knew where to draw the line. There were many challenges but they tackled them together as a united family. He was adored by his parents who wanted nothing but the best for him. They sent him to a multiracial private school in Bethlehem where he shared most classes with Bangani.

After doing matric, he went to the University of the Free State in Bloemfontein where he completed his Digital Marketing Course. A degree which came in handy for the ministry as he sourced innovative ways to engage the church youth in fun activities that ensured that they are financially taken care of. Outside of the house, Letlotlo was treated indifferently with the rest of the youth as they were all spiritually mentored closely by the people who loved them as though they were their own biological children.

When arriving in Clarens, the Makhethes had not given up trying for more children, but all efforts were in vain. Letlotlo was the only child they were blessed with. Which made their love for him as devotional as their commitment to faithfully serving

God, who adequately blessed them with many spiritual children in their ministry.

2.

Inside a cosy two bedroomed apartment that overlooked scenic mountains with estate houses, Bangani and Ithabeleng were sipping *Popular* red wine in their pyjamas on the couch. The rich flavourful aroma of macaroni and cheese with hints of herbs and chutney tantalized the open plan living room. They were both relaxed, sharing a teal throw. Bangani slightly tilted her head against the support of the back of her velvet sea green sofa while Ithabeleng was fully lying on her back, resting her head on the cushioned arm of the couch with her wine glass hardly leaving her lips.

The tumble dryer whirled in the background near the dishwasher, slow jams playing on the DVD player on the mounted chestnut TV stand which displayed a selection of DVD, CDs and Books. The great sounds of Frank Sinatra created an ambient mood, perfect for the kind of discussion that they were having.

An eerie glow from the Apollo light further in the distance infiltrated through the cream see-through curtain, complementing the almost invisible bulbs carved behind the framed African sculptures hanging on the wall. There were four of them; three on the wall opposite the couch, separated by a few centimetres and one between the entrance and the kitchen space.

"I can't exactly say no, *mmata*. Whatever you have lined up for me, is what I will explore." Bangani's voice sounded a bit unsure of what she was agreeing to.

"Gregory is a catch. He is one of the most eligible bachelors around, most likely to be your type. Sexy, confident and adventurous stud with a pretty smart head above his shoulders. I've confirmed that we'll join him and his crew for the White River rafting on Saturday afternoon."

"Oh dear, I haven't been to that river since - I don't even remember when! How cold is the water?"

"Seriously? Late September and you worry about the temperature of the water? *Wena mmata*, who used to scuba dive in the frosty cape aquatic?"

"I'm just taking precautionary measures. I wouldn't want this Gregory guy to think I'm a damsel in distress when I shiver from cold."

"Then you have every reason to, because that's a whole scenario right there. An op for him to cup you in his masculine arms."

"Does the poor guy know what misery he has gotten himself into?" Bangani shot a worried look at Ithabeleng who had not a single worry in her mind. Just mischievous plans of her own, visible through her devious grin. Her eyes glinted in thought.

"His entire entourage is quite intriguing, it makes me drool. I can't wait to be charmed as I admire each bicep when they paddle."

"I foresee an accident waiting to occur, aren't we also supposed to paddle? Then tell me how and where you're going to find balance between gauging the guys' muscles and controlling the raft simultaneously."

Ithabeleng laughed. "*Hao nthweo feela?* Those guys will take care of us. What are the guides for? This will give Gregory a chance to be your knight in shining armour."

 "Whatever! I just want to get this over and done with." Bangani dismissed the date that loomed to turn disastrous. She had plans of her own. Plans that excited her.

"It's not that simple darling, you still have to kiss plenty of frogs before you meet your royal prince. I hear Zac was adamant with his terms. From the lined up squad, we still haven't found the one who's the obvious royal. Meaning you better be prepared to get personal with each on the first encounter."

"What do you mean 'lined up squad?'"

"Nothing. You will see as the week unfolds."

"Ithabeleng Snyman, you will confess this very moment. It's my life we're talking about here. Come on! Out with it."

"Okay, okay! Relax. It's just Gregory on Saturday. He will bring a couple of his friends also. Then it's Kabelo, you'll spend Sunday morning with him - fishing trout."

"And?"

"Then there's Lawrence for next week Saturday and Thabang whom you stood up for Karaoke night. You'll see him next week Thursday."

"Lawrence, the owner of this wine?" she pointed with her eyes raising the glass in her hand.

"The one and only. He's dying to meet you and I'm sure you'll have plenty to discuss with your wine experience."

"Trust me, I'll only go for the free drinking spree. He is a nerd, I'll be bored to death *hle mmata*, I'm sure *le wena* you know that."

"Beggars can't be choosers, sister! I'm just saying go out with them and see what can be established from these dates. You still get to decide if they qualify for call-backs."

"I suppose." She took a sip from her almost empty glass, then she remembered something and she freaked.

"Hang on, did you say wine tasting is next Saturday?"

"Yes, why?"

"I'm afraid I can't. I won't make it."

"What do you mean you won't?" Ithabeleng frowned.

"We'll just have to reschedule. I'm attending the youth conference."

"*Mmata*, are you seriously going to postpone a private wine tasting, courtesy of the smoking hot owner of the winery for the boring youth conference?"

"It's not just for the boring conference silly, it's the date with Tlotla. Technically, it is still part of the mission."

"Oh! I can't believe hunky Lawrence is losing to the lame church boy."

"He is not lame. Your hunky Lawrence will get his turn. I'm sure he will understand that I am quite *popular*." They both laughed and drank from their glasses. Bangani got off the couch to place the empty glass on the dolphin coaster on the chrome glass coffee table. She yawned and stretched, accentuating her abs and toned obliques underneath her skewed white and teal pyjama top.

"Aren't you getting us another bottle?"

"Have you looked at the time? It's way past 11PM, we still have to jog tomorrow morning. And I have a hectic day ahead. Roxanne mixed up the prices, and I was too disturbed to scold her. I simply told her that we'd do them first thing in the morning."

"You're such a party pooper. I am not jogging, so I will drink that bottle, thank you very much."

Ithabeleng stood up to the mini bar that separated the kitchen and the dining room. Her physique clearly needs the workout, which she always postpones. Who would dare tell 'Miss Opinionated' that she is bursting?

"Be my guest. Sweet dreams." Bangani walked past Ithabeleng and disappeared in her bedroom but left the door slightly opened.

"Good night, love. I can't wait for you to meet Lawrence so that we stack up the wine rack. You're almost out." She yelled.

Bangani, called out in a huskier voice from her bedroom. "*Mos,* you're the one who exploits my wine, you stack it up. Every time you sleep over we down two bottles."

"Whatever!" Ithabeleng murmured.

"I heard that!" Bangani shouted.

***

Mama Jerry opened the grey thick curtains that revealed crystal white lace to let in a beam of light, saturating the bedroom that morning. Wearing a white *doek,* peach and white night gown, the ray of light reflected off her warm face. It clearly indicated that she was ageing gracefully. Because she had no courage to wake her husband, who seemed to be pretty relaxed in *la la land,* on a king-sized bed with a mahogany headboard with his Bible, notebook and pen by the bedside lamp, she relied on the brightness to do the honours.

Indeed, Pastor Jerry reacted accordingly as light penetrated. He half sleepily covered his eyes with his hands until he finally brought himself up to wake up from the cosy white linen.

"Good morning, daddy. I didn't mean to wake you." She said softly, almost apologetically.

He yawned and smiled lazily.

"Good morning, love. You make a terrible liar, you know? That's your oldest trick."

She laughed guiltily. "Okay, you caught me. Don't you always! How did you sleep, my love?"

"Ah! No new visions. I suppose God wants me to rest of late. Clearly you have something on your mind, spit it out." He brought himself up to rest on the continental pillow.

"I couldn't help but notice that you and Tlotla were in some intense discussion yesterday. What seems to be bothering our son?"

"I knew that it was just a matter of time before this question came. Aren't you too predictable, wifey? Our son is bothered by a woman."

"You don't say, love. Anyone in particular?"

"Bangani Khumalo."

"You're not referring to Bangani from the Curio Shop, *akere* daddy?" she was startled.

"In the flesh. At least she's the only one I know of. Why do you seem alarmed?"

"I had always thought he'd pick any of the beautiful flowers from the committed servants. Not some random girl who does not even notice when the church seating arrangement has changed."

"Come now, love. That's very mean, and judgemental."

"I'm sorry, but it's the truth. Don't you find it strange that since her grandmother passed on, she can hardly count to five the times she's set foot in the church?"

"There is nothing wrong with that. She was raised well. I believe she would bring amusement to Letlotlo. He truly loves her."

"But daddy…"

He interrupted her. "But nothing mama, the boy has made his choice. All that's left is for you and I to support him wholeheartedly."

"His choice? You make it sound like it's the final call. He doesn't plan on marrying her, does he?" She was bewildered by this revelation.

"He seems pretty determined. Who knows?" he sounded convinced.

"I hope you did not encourage him, love."

"Believe you me, he doesn't need any encouragement."

"Lord, what have I done? Why are you punishing me? Please guide my son into the path of righteousness." She uttered a genuine prayer.

"Love, calm down. The boy is mature, I'm sure he wouldn't make a rush decision against God's will. Besides, what if Bangani is who God chose for him?"

"It's clear that you are spiritually resting. Pastor Jerry! Wake up, please!" She grimaced and stormed out of the bedroom and closed the door on him. He looked at the books by his side and took one where he writes his dreams and visions and he scribbled.

***

Letlotlo lingered in bed drowsily although alert. He laid flat, reminiscing about his encounter with his crush the previous day. His mind wandered to when their gazes met and their fingers touched. An electric spark sent arousal to his manhood and he grinned boyishly like a love-struck teenager.

Yes! I will marry you. These words reverberated in his mind. Immersed in a jolly mood, he tightly cuddled his blue and brown pillow that matched the bedding set and curtains. His mother had tried the curtain trick but he pretended as though he was fast asleep.

After she had left, Letlotlo browsed his room with half opened eyes and smiled to himself.

Yes! I will marry you, Tlotla. Oh man! If only wishes were horses, beggars would indeed ride.

He had always loved Bangani, and as a regular at her shop, he had seen her million times, but the kind of feeling he had had from that sultry Thursday afternoon was indescribably magical. For the first time, he felt, and even got the conviction, that the feelings between them could actually be mutual. He pinched himself so hard he almost caused a lesion on his thigh. He was grateful that Bangani had eventually broken the ice and teased to give way to the first move, which he was ready to project.

He could barely wait for the conference where he would make a bold move and show her how committed and devoted he was. He wished he could devise a reason to go to the Curio Shop before the conference. The week long wait loomed like a gruesome torture to him. He knew for a fact that he would not survive it. *You will be strong!* She had said. He was Letlotlo Makhethe, he had to.

***

Packing her black and yellow water suit inside a light blue and white beach bag, Bangani was half attentive as she ignored her ringing phone on the white scatter cushion that complimented the lavender standard and methylated spirit purple continental pillows neatly displayed on her white bed cover.

As she folded the blue beach towel, she brought it up close and smelled its floral scent closing her eyes. She quickly brought it down to be packed away into the bag, irritated that it did not carry the scent that she longed for. Her father's sunscreen lotion. She remembered how she robbed Zachariah out of that towel and traded her pink one. The mineral cucumber and lemon fragrance of the lotion always lingered for so long even when he had gone back to the Netherlands. It had always managed to inevitably bring him closer in a flash. She bit her bottom lip trying to stop the stinging tears that formed at that memory.

Cheer up, princess. Zachariah would say. She forbade the tears from falling. Her father hated to see her sad. In his loving memory, she lived each day seeking and crafting something that would cheer her up on a daily basis.

It had been over a month since they had buried him. She had had to be strong as it was a state funeral and she was expected to make a speech as neither Mildred nor Kate were fit for it. Little Nathan and Nathaniel were out of the question as they themselves did not understand what the commemoration was about in their father's absence. She remembered how the four year olds happily yelled at the pictures of their father that were projected on a slide show and she led out a chuckle. She wished she were as oblivious to pain as her half-brothers. Her heart went out as she travelled in future and witnessed how broken the twins would be, going forth without their father.

Zachariah was many things; devoted to his family and kickass at his job. The twins had missed out on the opportunity to learn so much from him. This steered a turmoil of emotions in her. She refrained from over-thinking about her father in fear of a meltdown.

He had demanded that she be married into a royal family. A request she was determined to fulfil. At all costs. Even if it meant going on million disastrous dates. Starting with the one she had with... *Gregory!*

The thought of Gregory brought her back to life. She abruptly stuffed the towel and sunscreen into the bag and reached for her phone. Panic hit her when she realised that she had lost track of time. She had three missed calls from Ithabeleng. She did not call her back, instead, she grabbed the beach bag and took one glance at her reflection in the mirror and almost dashed out... *This is the first date, mmata. You have to be dazzling!* Ithabeleng's warning voice came through in her head and she returned to take a full inspection in the mirror.

In a pair of white cotton shorts that accentuated her toned toffee coloured long and smooth legs, a coral tank top that hugged her in the right places - showing off her flat tummy and a sexy cleavage protruded in a decent manner. The navy and mint Ipanema flip-flops did justice to her pedicure. She had ash blonde and dark grey braids styled to one side to bring out her natural beauty with a subtle touch of makeup.

She reached for a vanity bag and took out a wine coloured glossy lipstick. After applying it on the bottom lip, she dabbed the top lip lightly to absorb the lipstick from the bottom one. When she was satisfied with this look, she pouted a few kisses and closed the bedroom door behind her.

***

It was almost dark outside when Bangani hastily pulled off her Jeep into the driveway of the sequence of flats where she was renting. She stormed out of the car, slammed the door and loped to her flat. Ithabeleng tiptoed after her trying to calm her down.

"*Mmata*, I'm so sorry that this turned out nasty. We shouldn't have gone to the club." Ithabeleng bellowed as she caught up with her at the entrance of the door while she struggled with the key.

"Sorry *ya eng, mmata?* It's not your fault that Gregory's so called entourage turned out to be a bunch of assholes after a few shots."

"That's why I say you and Gregory should have had your private outing."

"No, it's a blessing in disguise that we headed for Andy's. Else I'd have allowed things to get far, until late. Thinking that he was perfect."

"Wasn't he?" Ithabeleng searched Bangani's gaze for answers.

The door finally opened and they both went inside. Bangani dropped the keys in the wired sieve bowl on the kitchen table. Ithabeleng put both their beach bags on the floor near the washing machine. She looked at Bangani in the eye inquisitively.

"Personally? I thought he was quite a gentleman." She started off a little sensitive and got heated when adding, "It's his squad that turned me off and I can't get past their derogatory comments about that waitress."

"Never mind those losers. Are you and Greg going out again soon?"

"Why the hell would I do that?"

"Come on, love. Just because his friends can't handle themselves well when intoxicated doesn't mean you have to put off a good thing brewing between the two of you. It's not like he condoned their behaviour."

"What if he was doing it for a show? Who knows if he wouldn't have been the one who started it had we not been there?"

"But, we're not sure that..." Ithabeleng did not get the chance to finish her reasoning.

"But nothing!" Bangani interrupted. "A friend of a thief is a thief. And taking how highly he spoke of them, it's clear his life revolves around their brotherhood. I won't be the one to break that up."

"That's true. They'd call you a witch that came between them. For what it's worth, you and Greg would have made a great couple."

"If he was royal, I would maybe fight for a relationship. But you heard for yourself."

"His loss then." Ithabeleng accepted defeat. She switched on the coffeemaker and opened the cupboard. "I'm making coffee and then I'll get these wet things cleaned up."

"Thank you, coffee is what we need after downing those shots."

"Yep, for a good night sleep, missy. You have a date with KB tomorrow, remember?"

"How could I forget? Shoot me right now!"

3.

Bangani took a sip from her thick blueberry and beetroot smoothie and placed the squeeze jug on the counter top. She clicked on the designs on her laptop. It was a calm and warm morning and she appreciated the quiet to gather her thoughts while browsing through the designs. When looking for inspiration, a tranquil atmosphere was what she treasured.

Suddenly, two silhouettes appeared from outside and she raised her head to welcome the customers in. Her heart skipped a beat when she saw that it was not just anyone. Yes, in the flesh. It was Letlotlo and Mama Jerry. She yearned to find the hole to hide in.

"Good morning, Mrs. Makhethe." She bravely greeted with a huge smile looking into Mama Jerry's eyes. A bit unsettled by her unfathomable expression, she turned to Letlotlo and found him coyly admiring her. "Lovely to have you both here." She continued.

"How are you doing, BK?" *because I for one am not doing that well.* Letlotlo asked genuinely.

"I couldn't be better. Thank you for asking. I love Mondays." She lied. "How have you been?" She asked, looking at him quizzically.

He looked so sexy in blue jeans and a yellow golf shirt that had the church emblem on the left breast. His neatly combed black hair shone under the reflection of the headlamp. *God, he is so handsome!* His blushing moist lips curled into a smile and she realized how aware of him she had been. She smiled back avoiding eye contact.

"Good! Very good actually." He also lied. *I have been missing you terribly.*

"How was the church service, Mrs. Makhethe?" She tried not to stare straight into her eyes this time.

"It was lovely, thank you! Psalm 84:10 says 'One day spent in His Temple is better than a thousand anywhere else.' How did you spend your Sunday, Bangani?" She probed self-righteously, looking into her eyes.

"Oh, I was working all weekend. I have been swamped for days." With her eyes dancing out of place, she lied again. *Why am I lying?* She smiled through fighting her inner voice. *You can't exactly tell them that you have been out all weekend, drinking like a fish with different men.*

"I see." Mama Jerry said flatly.

No you don't. Bangani wanted to blurt out, feeling judged. She forged a smile. A smile that widened when she looked at Letlotlo.

"You work too hard, BK. A little rest is necessary once in a while." He said, concerned.

"No rest for the hustlers. What can I do for you today?"

"Actually my son is here on my account, I asked him to bring me here. He was raving all weekend about your work." Mama Jerry said, perkily grabbing his arm, almost possessively.

"Did he?" Bangani asked vibrantly.

"Of course. Why are you acting so surprised? It's no secret how much I love your work. Mama and daddy also loved the key holders."

"Yes, we did. Which is why I've come to ask if you can do something for me as well. The church ladies and I are going away for our annual end of the year function in December. Tlotla advised we come as early as possible to give you time to work your magic."

"Sounds wonderful. I'll be happy to help. And he was right to ask you to place an order on time."

"I thought so. You always say: 'art is not to be rushed.'" He mimicked her and they burst into laughter.

"Someone has been paying attention. I'm impressed." She winked at him. She turned to Mama Jerry who was too quick to gather her seriousness after letting out a chuckle. "What do you have in mind, Mrs. Makhethe?"

"Oh, dear! I was thinking you would be able to advise me on what to get. I want a memorable token. Something meaningful, that won't wear off after some time."

"Something eternal?" Bangani added searchingly.

"Definitely something eternal!" Mama Jerry beamed.

"Let me leave you two to get down to the nitty-gritty and check out what's new." He left them alone, delighted that they had found common ground.

"Well, do you think you can come up with something that the ladies will treasure eternally?"

"Um. Actually I have a few ideas. Where are you going? Maybe we can do something that resonates with the place itself."

"Maliba Lodge in Lesotho. I'm sorry I don't have much detail about the place that could spark your inspiration."

"In Tsehlanyane? What a beautiful place with picturesque mountains and a river that flows peacefully!" Bangani jaunted dreamily.

"You have been? Tlotla showed us the website and the ladies did not hesitate to confirm the booking. It looked surreal."

"Trust me, the website doesn't do it justice. The location in itself is infinitely memorable. You're all going to have a jovial time there."

"Now you want me to dread why it had to be so far in December." Mama Jerry loosened.

"I'm sorry. December is actually perfect as it will be during the rainy season and the mountains will be so green that broccoli wouldn't match. And the river will be flowing acutely and soundly as the rushing water hits upon the rocks. A mere thought and I am already jealous that I won't be there."

They both chuckled loudly. Letlotlo appeared to ensure that he was not imagining things. When he realized that they did not even notice him, he went back to the book aisle and paged a few books.

"That can be arranged, you just impress the ladies with their gifts and they will welcome you with open arms. We are one another's rock in the union."

"I will do my best to win their hearts through my art."

"Good! Did you know that your grandmother founded the group? Back then when we were so young and needed guidance from her and other wise women of noble character."

"You don't say! I honestly didn't know. Wow! Thank you so much, Mrs. Makhethe." She was emotionally touched. Any project that had an element of her grandmother got her fully invested.

"You are welcome, child. And please call me Mama Jerry." She was surprised at herself for having been so comfortable.

"Mama Jerry. You have given me something to work on. Before the end of this week you will have your design ready and upon your approval we can start with the actual gifts. Tell me. How many are you?"

"We are a group of thirty; twenty old ladies and ten young women. But let's make the order for thirty-five, just to cater for surplus should more women be interested in joining us."

"I'm definitely going to be one of them."

"Good, your grandmother would be so proud." Mama Jerry nodded approvingly.

"I can't wait to get started, my creative juices are already flowing. Once done with the first draft, I'll send it to Tlotla and he can show it to you. Or you can take my card and send me your contact details."

"I heard my name." Letlotlo approached with a purple and pink bible cover and a grey and white one, flashing them in front of his mother's eyes, seeking approval.

"I was telling Mama Jerry, that I'll send you the design once done or she…"

"Yes! Please do send it to me." Letlotlo pleaded cheerfully. The thought of receiving a message from Bangani gave him expected joy. When he saw that he had invited prying eyes he added reassuringly, "Mama and phones aren't the best of friends. By the time she sees it, it will be too late, and you BK would have lost your marbles, dying for feedback."

"He's got a point. Let's use his phone." Mama Jerry agreed.

"That settles it then. I'm cool with that." Bangani chirped in.

"Do send the invoice as well." Mama Jerry pleaded.

"Oh, that will only be sorted once we know the material to be used. After you authorize the design I will draft it and we'll go over it in person."

"Thank you, dear."

"I'm glad you two found a mutual agreement. What do you think of these covers, mommy dearest?"

"Aren't they lovely! Have you seen how worn out your father's is?"

"I can personalise them for you if you prefer." Bangani offered.

"Aren't you an angel! I'd appreciate it so much." Letlotlo emitted.

"Only if it's not too much work, we don't want to distract you from other urgent projects." Mama Jerry sounded unsure.

"Not at all, Mama. You just tell me what to write and I will do it in a split second. If you are in a hurry, you can leave the ink to dry and Tlotla can come later to collect them."

"Perfect. How much are they?"

"No, mom! Don't rob me of my blessings. This is my treat."

"Thank you, my boy!" She smiled at him and gave him a squeeze on his cheeks.

"You can scribble here." Bangani handed them a notepad and pen. She left them to decide while she went to welcome a young couple that had walked in.

After Letlotlo wrote his parents' names, he ushered his mother out of the shop and gave a reassuring look to Bangani that he would be coming back.

***

Bangani was already in bed when Letlotlo's call came through. She was not pleased that they did not get their most sought after privacy when he came to collect the Bible covers. She was busy with clients and Roxanne had just returned from the bank. She had yearned to see him. Be with him. He was growing on her.

Letlotlo had not been able to hide his irritation when he found that she had company and they looked very occupied. He pretended he was in as much hurry as others and simply took the gift bag from Bangani, swiped his card, and without wasting another minute, he was out of the shop.

"Oh! but you had my mother eating out of the palm of your hands. You should give me tips." He teased over the phone.

"No, I did not! She intimidates me so much!" Bangani confessed.

"I noticed that she was a bit unsociable when we first..."

"A bit?" She hurled in. "That's an understatement of note. I've never felt so tiny. She brought back the trauma of being called into Mrs. Watson's office when we'd done something naughty back then." They both laughed.

"BK, you are exaggerating. My mom is nothing compared to Mrs. Watson. That woman was pure evil!"

"Maybe I should remind you that she actually quoted a scripture to make me feel like I was gallivanting instead of going to church. I've never felt so unrighteous."

"I am sorry she made you feel that way. But you put her in her place. Tell me, what did you do?"

She giggled "I did no such thing. We just clicked when discussing the project."

"I couldn't believe my ears when I heard the two of you laughing out so loudly. None of you even noticed that I peeped to confirm."

"You did? We did not see you."

"My point exactly, you were so thrown by whatever mutual ground you found. She wouldn't stop telling daddy about you. To his disbelief."

"And the covers? Everyone happy?"

"They loved them. Thank you."

"Don't mention it."

"I owe you so many favours now, I wonder how am I ever going to repay you."

"I could think of a few ways." She teased flirtingly. "But they're going to cost you big time."

"I love a challenge." He affirmed confidently.

"Good. I can be very demanding. So be prepared."

"Whatever you wish for, I will make it happen. In fact, I'd be honoured."

"Listen to yourself, trying to flatter me. Letlotlo Makhethe, you have no idea what you just got yourself into. Good night."

"Sweet dreams." *Dream about us*. He wanted to say. But she hung up. She did mention that she was already in bed.

Letlotlo was lying on top of his blankets, sheepishly savouring every bit of that moment. Now that he had spoken with his love, he would sleep like a baby. He was smitten!

4.

"Oh dear, what do we have here!"

Mama Jerry exclaimed. She was looking at the 3D presentation on Bangani's laptop.

A pebble engraved thus:

Upon this rock,

I will build my church.

~*Matthew 16:18*

"You like it?" Bangani enquired solemnly.

"I love it! It's perfect." Reassured Mama Jerry, shocked at Bangani's modesty.

"I'm glad you love it. It meant so much working on it, especially after you told me about Mani Zandi's contribution."

"That explains it. It's evident that you took your heart out, child. Even I didn't think you'd come up with something so profound." Mama Jerry uttered.

"You did mention that you ladies are one another's rock. Tsehlanyane river is lavished with dark beautiful rocks, that's a lifetime memory nugget."

"You even paid extra attention, my child. I said that in passing, I didn't think you'd incorporate it with the project."

"Artists are always attentive to detail, no matter how small."

"Well, I'm delighted. You came highly recommended. I thought it was because my son is in love with you. You did a magnificent job."

"I was also thinking, we can pierce through the rock and add a beaded necklace to make it a pendant rock." She continued raving passionately, unconscious of the confession.

"Brilliant! Let's do it."

"Every time any of you wear it, you will all be reminded that women are rocks, and that you represent the church of Christ."

"Eternal symbol. Thank you so much, my child. Gogo Zandi would have been so proud of you."

That was Bangani's cue. She broke into an emotional sob. Yes, she knew that her grandmother would be so proud of her. Not only that, she had just heard that Letlotlo is in love with her. She had been dying to hear this. She had felt it. And fought it. Futilely so. She wondered if her grandmother would approve of him. On that thought, she was enveloped by a peace that she had not felt in a long time.

When Mama Jerry saw how emotional she got, she gave her a tight squeeze on the shoulder and cupped the hand that was freely on the cordless mouse.

"I'm sorry, mama." She sniffed away the tears. "I didn't mean to break down like that."

"It's alright, my baby." Mama Jerry leaned towards her so that Bangani would rest her head on her shoulder.

She sniffed and smiled. "These are happy tears. I've never felt so close to her. In this very room. Her aura is thickly present."

"She lives in us, my child. She's multiplied herself in all of us. Do you know how much you take after her? Your wisdom is proof that she influences you still. Especially on this project."

"Thank you for your comforting words, mama."

"My son is very blessed to have you. I am sorry that I was not open to the idea at first. You are a remarkable young lady, Bangani."

Bangani's gut tightened. She felt a lump in her throat. It only dawned to her. *You have to quit games, Bangani. Before someone gets hurt.*

She sniffed and smoothly broke loose of Mama Jerry's tight grip. She suddenly became professional. "I will get on with the work right away, mama. I might have to go to Maliba Lodge as soon as possible. To handpick the pebbles from the river. That way it will not cost an arm and leg to produce."

"Oh dear, the invoice! Please don't worry about the costs, my child. Tlotla and I will wire an EFT as soon as you send it through."

"Absolutely not. I will not allow you to pay for this one." Bangani protested.

"No, Bangani. You are running a business here, don't feel guilt trapped to do this for free. The church is not here to take advantage of you. We will pay."

"Mama Jerry, please hear me. This project brought me ultimate healing and peace of mind. Please accept my offering."

"On one condition." Reasoned Mama Jerry when she saw that Bangani's mind was made up.

"Anything, mama."

"You will allow Tlotla to drive you there."

Bangani broke into a cold sweat. The thought of spending so much time alone with Letlotlo. At a picturesque Maliba Lodge. *Oh God, I will not survive it.* Heat rose to her plumpy cheeks and she felt mushy in the gut. "I don't..." she tried to protest.

"I am not taking no for an answer. Don't even try to battle this one. It's a lost case."

Mama Jerry expressed sternly and grabbed her handbag from the counter top. In a blink of an eye, she was at the door and out.

***

Bangani locked herself in her bedroom the minute she got in. She took precaution knowing that Ithabeleng had a spare key to her flat. She did not want to see anyone. Or speak to anyone for that matter. Not even her best friend and favourite cousin. She wanted to be alone. She had not even pleaded with Roxanne to get the rest of the afternoon off. She demanded it. When Roxanne dared to protest, Bangani threatened that she would lose her job.

She was grateful for her en-suit bathroom as she would avoid Ithabeleng peacefully if she decided to come. After thrusting her belongings on the bed, she pell-mell to run a quick shower. Within seconds, she was out. She dived into bed and covered herself.

She had had an emotionally draining day. Her feelings were all over the place. She needed to deal with that in peace. *What peace? You have caused havoc. He is in love with you.*

She wondered how she would tell Letlotlo that they can't be together. This broke her because she knew that he was not just a casual fling. A pastor's son his age. *I'm sure his parents are already planning a wedding and thinking of christening names for our kids. Bangani Khumalo, what have you done?*

The thought of marriage and kids brought a peculiar elation. Not so long ago, this was the last thing on her mind. All this time when she mocked the dates that Ithabeleng suggested, she had thought that if anyone met the criteria required by Zachariah's Will, it would only be a transactional marriage. No love or emotions invested. She had been okay with it like that.

The thought of being married to Letlotlo was a different matter altogether. It was something she sincerely yearned for. *Since when Bangani?* Since she found out he is in love with her. And his parents approve. *He is in love with me.*

This brought joy and fear at the same time. *Am I falling in love too?* She laughed at the absurd thought.

5.

When Bangani stepped out of her flat that sunny Saturday morning, Letlotlo was convinced that he was seeing an angel. Draped in a white floating skater dress, braids neatly tied into a bun with a white floral scrunch ribbon, and white and gold sandal with a high thick and rounded heel, she looked like she had just stepped off a Hollywood celebrity red carpet.

"It's rude to stare." She ridiculed when she approached Letlotlo leaning outside a classic red Mercedes AMG 4matic.

Taken aback, Letlotlo staggered towards her managing a smile. "Can you blame me? You look like a dream." He uttered almost breathlessly.

"Oh stop it, you're making me nervous. I'm sorry I kept you waiting." She leaned to hug him. The sweet notes of vanilla and musk almost concealed the spicy sandalwood but highlighted apple cinnamon and gave it the novelty to saturate the air. Although she broke off the embrace quicker than he imagined, the fragrance enticed and sent a rush of heat to his senses.

"You look... breathtakingly gorgeous. You smell beautiful. You..." He ran out of words just in time for her to interrupt him.

"Stop it. You don't look too shabby yourself. Now, are we going to spend the entire day on this parking lot or is the conference maybe cancelled?"

"Oh, sorry. You took my breath away. I've never seen you prettier. And I'm thinking, what could I have possibly done to deserve such grace."

He quickly rushed to open the passenger door gesturing her in. He patiently waited for her to climb on.

"Thank you." She smiled as he closed the door and rushed to open his door. Without wasting any moment, he turned on the ignition of the German machine and they were out in a jiffy.

Later in the evening, Bangani invited Letlotlo for coffee. But as soon as they closed the door, coffee was the last thing on their minds.

"Do you have any idea how I have longed for this moment?" He said, leaning closer to look her deeply into her brown eyes. Her makeup was still flawless and the scarlet lipstick fresh from the reapplication she did after refreshments at the conference. He knew this because he had not let her out of his side, despite having been disturbed several times by the event organiser who sought his approval on every little detail.

"You have? Maybe you can show me just..." she said as her lips invitingly curved into a smile.

If he had reserved any patience, it betrayed him at that very moment. He gently pressed his lips against hers, cupping her closer to him. An erotic heat sparked between them as their bodies collided in a tidal wave of passion. Equally yearning, she welcomed this burning surge of hunger for desire as she patently responded to his demand. A moment, maybe two passed as they shared a slow, deep and passionate kiss. She had not felt anything like it. She wrapped her hands around his neck to enclose him, grateful that her heels supported her height and kept him at a length she appreciated. He smiled lovingly as they broke the kiss at the same time. She smiled back without opening her eyes to savour the moment. He planted a soft longing kiss on her forehead.

"You are beautiful! Do you know that?" He murmured as he lowered his head to claim her with a kiss. She nodded in a smile, gesturing him to the couch. Taking a hint, he obediently swept her off her feet and in a split second, he had kicked off both their shoes. They laid side to side on the velvet sofa. They hungrily devoured each other in a long paced kiss. When she felt his bulging desire, she broke into a cold sweat.

What do you think you are doing? An inner voice rebuked her and she abruptly broke from the kiss. Alarmed, he frowned in disbelief. "Is something wrong?"

"No... Yes! I don't know, Tlotla."

"You are not making any sense, darling." When she distanced herself from him, he guiltily sat up and searched her gaze. "I will not take advantage of you, my love. I am a patient man, if that's what worries you. Tonight I just wanted to taste those red tempting lips. Nothing more, I promise."

"It's not that. If anyone is taking advantage here, it ought to be me. But it's not that."

"What is it then?" Letlotlo was confused.

"We can't. I can't lead you on. Nothing can come out of this. And I don't want to hurt you."

"Hurt me how, BK? And what do you mean lead me on? I am not blind. In fact, all my senses are perfectly working. We both feel this. Don't we?" He questioned.

"Yes, it's magical. But we can't. I am sorry." She sniffed away runny mucus.

"Why do you keep apologising? Hey. What's the matter? Don't be sad."

"Why not? This is a hopeless situation." She broke into tears. He felt pity and his heart went out to her. Confused as he was, he edged closer and cupped her into an embrace.

"I am not going anywhere, darling. I have loved you all my life. Tonight I love you even more and I want to spend the rest of my life with you."

"Just stop, Tlotla." She wailed loudly now and he became even more frustrated.

"It's true. All of it." He professed.

"This stops tonight. We can't be. You are not royal."

"What do you mean? Will you quit the riddles?"

She looked at him and it broke her to see the love in his eyes. It was evident. She had felt it in every touch and every passing moment of their kiss. *Tell him! If you love him, let him go.*

"I can't be with you, Tlotla. Circumstances don't allow me." She sniffed away the tears and attempted to speak steadily. "I have to honour my father's wishes. He requested me to marry into a royal family."

Letlotlo loosened and smiled.

"Why are you smiling?"

"Weren't you at the conference with me earlier? The Kingdom principles? I am as royal as royalty can be, darling." He said confidently.

She looked confused. "I mean royal royal, Tlotla. This is no joke."

"I am not joking either. Because my Father is the King of Glory. Do I really have to recite 1 Peter chapter 2 to you? Isaiah 62:3! You were there with me, my love. I could go on and on, but I'll just bore you with countless scriptures that you know of."

She couldn't help it but laugh. "You don't understand. I don't mean church royalty. I mean by blood, by monarchy, true royalty."

Letlotlo realized that they were not on the same page. He did not have the strength to validate his

Christianity. Not tonight. Especially not to her. He thought she understood, and it disappointed him that she did not see his perspective. *How could I have been so mistaken?*

"I have to go." He stood up and grabbed his keys. He was shattered. He could not stand to be insulted further than that. He left in a distraught state and closed the door behind him.

She was left devastated. Alone. She sank her head on the cushion and cried.

***

When he got home, Letlotlo's parents were watching the youth conference recording on his laptop. He greeted them in a low voice and walked past them. Immediately, Mama Jerry saw that he was not himself.

"Tlotla, are you okay? What's wrong my boy?"

"Nothing. I'm just tired. Good night."

"Son, well done with the service. You pulled a great symposium indeed." Pastor Jerry said, still looking at the laptop.

"Thanks, daddy."

"Love, don't you see that Tlotla is distraught? How was your date?"

"Sorry, son. I had forgotten."

"I am really tired, let's talk tomorrow please."

"No, son. You don't look too well. What happened?" his mother persuaded.

"I said nothing. Will you please stop nagging?" he yelled.

"Not in my house, son. You will apologise to your mother this second!"

"I am sorry. May I be excused please?"

"No! Your mother is worried about you. The least you can do is tell her what's bothering you. You were looking forward to your date with Bangani all week. Now you come back and bite our heads off. Explain yourself young man."

"Let it out, my baby. You can't go to bed angry. You can't give the devil that satisfaction."

"I am not angry. I am disappointed that's all."

"You and Bangani didn't hit it off?" Letlotlo would laugh at his father when he spoke informally. He often teased that if any member of the congregation caught them off-guard, they would be traumatised by his choice of words. Tonight his choice of words was not funny as much as it pierced a hole in his heart.

"I doubt. They are a match made in heaven." Mama Jerry reassured.

"If only. It's over even before it started."

"What do you mean, Tlotla? This can't be right. You two are perfect for each other." She disputed.

"Apparently not." Letlotlo said flatly.

"Did you fight on the first date?" his father asked.

"Worse. Everything was perfect. Until I found out that I am not what she is looking for."

"Is she out of her mind? Then why agree to go out with you if she doesn't like you?"

"I don't know, daddy. She says I'm not royal."

"What does she even mean by that?" Mama Jerry was perplexed.

"It's a long story. May I please, go to my room? I really need to be alone."

"Oh my baby, you don't deserve any of this."

"Son, there is nothing that is beyond the power of God. Speak to Him and He will guide you."

"Thanks, daddy. Good night mom. I love you both."

"Good night, son. We love you more." They chorused.

6.

"*Mmata!* Explain to me why you've been avoiding me all week? And it better be good. You don't even return my calls. You stood up Thabang for the second time. What am I going to do with you?"

Ithabeleng barged in yelling. She walked towards Bangani who was sleeping on the couch. She did not respond, nor look up. Instantly, Ithabeleng realised that something was amiss.

"Hey, sweetheart. What's wrong?"

Bangani sniffed and said nothing.

"Talk to me, love. I'm sorry I yelled." She sat down on the couch where Bangani laid, and she removed the throw, revealing that she was still in yesterday's outfit. She realised that she was still wearing makeup which was messy from crying.

"You slept here? Looks like you've been crying. Sweetheart, what happened?" Ithabeleng was moved by the state she found her in.

Bangani could not hold her tears any longer. She broke down into a wail. "I love him!"

“Who? The church boy?” Ithabeleng asked in disbelief. She leaned in to hug Bangani.

“Yes. I love him. With every fibre in my body.”

“That’s a good thing, *mmata.* Is that the reason why you’re crying?”

“How is it a good thing if we can’t be together?”

“What do you mean? Did he judge you?”

“It’s the other way round actually.” Bangani sat up straight. “I am the one with a condition.”

“Oh dear! Zac?” Ithabeleng asked knowingly. Bangani nodded and looked into the distance.

“I hate my father. I hate my life. I hate everything. It all sucks!” She cried.

“Stuff Zac and his absurd demands, *mmata.* It’s the first time I hear you say you love a man. Zac can’t control your life from the grave.”

“I can’t exactly defy him. I have to honour his last wish. Besides, I need that money. My business desperately needs it.”

“At the expense of your one chance at finding happiness and love?”

“It’s a sacrifice that I have to make. I just wonder if Tlotla will ever forgive me. I didn’t want to hurt him. You should have seen how quick he was to get out of here." She sniffed.

"I am going to run you a hot bubble bath. Then we are going to the spa. You will feel better afterwards." Ithabeleng gestured her to get off the couch as she took the throw from her.

Bangani did not argue. She got off and disappeared into her bedroom.

***

Letlotlo spent days in isolation. Interrogating God. Praying. Fasting. But nothing made sense. He had no answers.

His parents gave him the much sought after space. Hard as it was for his mother to keep her distance. She wanted to go to the curio shop and tell Bangani where to get off. No one was allowed to treat her son the way she did. Pastor Jerry put off her fire. He suggested they support their son in prayer.

On the seventh day of his prayer and fasting, Letlotlo had a peculiar dream. He dreamt of an old man whom he had never seen before. The man was frail from sickness. He looked at him and pleaded for his help. Letlotlo wanted to help this man but it looked like there was a barrier keeping them apart. There was a void and null space that had no ground that separated them. The old man kept on coughing and crying out Letlotlo's name. He tossed and turned in his sleep. The shouting became louder until he woke up and realised that his mother had just opened his door and was indeed calling him.

He woke up abruptly and looked at her. "Mom, you gave me a fright."

"I'm sorry, Tlotla. There is someone for you in the living room."

"Someone for me? Who could it be?"

"It's an old man, he didn't say much. He demanded to see you. Freshen up while I go prepare breakfast. Your fast ends today, right?"

"Yes, mom. I'll be there in five minutes."

"Okay, my baby." She said and left his room. He dawdled in bed for a while. He stretched his limbs and yawned, got off and made his bed as neatly as possible. Then he went to shower.

***

Kate was excited to see her daughter's call coming through. She was walking by the beach, waves crashing against the coral reef. She quickly picked it up excitedly.

"I still have a daughter! Lucky me!" she mocked playfully.

"Good morning, mother. How are you doing?"

"Now that I am talking to my favourite daughter? *Goed dankie.*"

"You mean your only daughter."

"Yes *liefie, hoe gaan dit?*"

"I am okay thanks. I just missed you." Bangani said in a deflated sigh.

"*Nie, my kind.* You can't lie to me. What is wrong?"

"Must you always psychoanalyse me, *ausi* Kate? Nothing is wrong."

"Bangani Khumalo, daughter of Kathrine and Zachariah. I was not born yesterday. *Kom nou*, out with it."

"Fine. I have failed to fulfil your darling Zachariah's wishes. And I give up." She sadly confessed.

"Okay. Slow down, baby. It's only been like a month or so? Give it time."

"I don't have the luxury of time. I have to watch my dream of expansion fall apart just like that."

"You mean there is not even a tiny bit of luck from all dates that Ithabeleng organised?"

"I did not go to all of them. It became exhausting. Dad can keep his money." She said in a firm voice.

"What else are you keeping from me, *my kind?*"

"Nix. I am just tired. Although the inheritance would have come in handy, securing it has taken way too much of my energy."

"And?" Kate knew that tone very well. Her daughter was not okay.

"And that's all. Why do you always want to make a big deal out of nothing."

"My hunch is never wrong, young lady. *Wat is sy naam?*"

"Whose name?"

"The boy who stole your heart?"

"There is no boy, and my heart is still in place."

"*My kind,* follow your heart. I will support you."

"He is not royal." She said despondently.

"Who cares? Are you in love with him?"

"More than you will ever know."

"Then what's stopping you? Zac's bloody money? You don't need it."

"But my business does, *ausi* Kate. There's no denying that fact"

"I wanted to wait until Christmas, but I'll say this now. I have a confession to make."

"What?"

"There is a gold fund that we opened with Zac when you were just a baby. We've been saving gold for your future. When you left CT, Zac and I planned to give you access in December."

"How much?" Bangani enquired happily.

"A lot! The inheritance and its condition is peanuts compared to what's in that vault."

"Wow, mother! You have watched me suffer; trying to build the curio shop and you conveniently forgot to tell me that I am a trust fund baby?"

"Not just any trust fund, *my kind*. Physical gold. With the depreciation of fiat currency, your investment has only gotten fatter with time. Even more that I anticipated."

"Wow! This is the best news ever! Thank you, thank you, thank you so much, mom!"

"I know, so you see there's no reason to... *wag 'n Bietjie*. Did you just call me, **mom**?"

"Yes, mom! After this great confession, you're literally the best mom ever!" Bangani beamed excitedly.

"Had I known that I would get this reaction, I'd have told you way sooner. But it was supposed to be your wedding gift. I was actually going to give it to you when you found the man of your father's dreams. He always said; gold is for kings and queens."

"Oh, now I get it! That explains why he insisted on me marrying royalty. I am terribly sorry to disappoint you both."

"*Nee my lief.* You have never disappointed me. I admire you. You were willing to walk away from your inheritance that came with strings attached in order for you to do you. That's bravery! In my books, that's even a better quality."

"It's not like I had a choice. I have failed dad, but it's okay. At least I tried. You win some, you lose some."

"So, when do I meet him? Your win."

"My loss, you mean? He hates me. He is disgusted by me. I lost him too." She admitted regrettably.

"You are not a loser. Go find that boy and be happy, *my kind*. No man would ever say no to you."

"I won't hold my breath. But I will try."

"Holding thumbs for you baby."

"*Dankie! Ek is lief vir jou ma.*" Bangani said energetically.

"I love you more, *my kind*. I'll speak to Harald about granting you access to the vault."

7.

Bangani wanted to break the news in person. She had yearned to see Letlotlo's phone notifications but none came. She gathered strength to go to his house. She was met by a hostile Mama Jerry, as intimidating as she was when she came to her shop. She silently prayed that Letlotlo could appear to her rescue. Instead, Pastor Jerry came to the living room where his wife was standing ready to attack. He offered Bangani a seat.

"She is not staying. She is not welcome here." Mama Jerry said firmly.

"Come on, mama. Let's hear the child out. Sit down, my daughter."

"Thank you, Pastor Jerry. Mama, I know I'm probably the last person you expected to see. But this is important. I have to see him. I owe him an apology."

"You broke my boy. And now you have the audacity to show your face here?"

"Mama, *ako butle hle*. What do you want to apologise for, my daughter?"

"For being an idiot. Can I see him please?"

"You're still an idiot to have come here, thinking your lousy apology will make things right. And the answer is no, you can't see him." Mama Jerry said angrily.

"Tlotla is in Lesotho, my daughter. He had personal business to attend to."

"Oh! Do you perhaps know when he will be back?"

"His whereabouts are none of your business. To think I actually gave you a chance. I should have just followed my gut and protected my son. Now we don't even know if he will ever set foot here again."

"Mama, it's not Bangani's fault that our son left. We knew that he could go back to his family anytime they found each other."

"What do you mean his family, Pastor?"

"It's her fault. Because if my son hadn't been so deeply hurt, he would have at least told us when he would be coming back."

"He didn't tell you that we adopted him? His biological father contacted him. We honestly did not know that he was still alive."

"No, he never mentioned it. Does it mean that I've lost him forever?"

"Serves you right, you were too self-righteous for him. How I regret our encouragement to pursue you. Now we have also lost him, and I will never forgive you for that."

"I am very sorry, mama. It was never my intention, I was confused."

"Was?" Pastor Jerry asked keenly.

"I came to right my wrongs. I love him and I was a fool to let him go."

"You love him? Wow! That is wonderful news, my daughter. He will be delighted to know."

"What's the point? He might not come back. I guess I should just accept my loss and go."

"That would be for the best." Mama Jerry professed.

"Don't give up, my daughter. Anything can happen." Assured Pastor Jerry.

"Thank you, Pastor. I will be off now. Mama Jerry, I hope one day you will find it in your heart to forgive me."

"Don't hold your breath. Only God knows."

"Go well, my daughter."

She hesitated, still hoping that Letlotlo would come out and confess that it was all a prank. She dragged her feet out and closed the door behind her. She felt Mama Jerry's scornful look but she did not bother to turn.

***

Ithabeleng and Bangani were stuffing themselves with ice cream. Bangani's head resting on Ithabeleng's lap on the sofa.

"Sweetheart, you've got to give yourself a break." Ithabeleng said, caressing her hair.

"It's confirmed, *mmata*. I should just go cat hunting already. My fate is clear."

"Oh come now! You don't believe that, do you?"

"How long have I been single? Tell me! The one man who loves me and worships the ground I walk on has gone AWOL on me. The one man that I am deeply in love with. I am a hopeless case.”

“It’s not the end of the world. You are young, successful, hot and a fabulous kickass artist and curator. You have so much to live for.”

“I get that, *mmata*. But what good is it if I spend my entire life alone?”

“Quit being cynical. You don’t know what the future holds. You came back to Clarens to find treasure. I believe treasure is about to find you, darling.” A knock on the door rapped through just as Ithabeleng was comforting her.

“I wonder who it could be.” Bangani looked confused as she was not expecting any company.

“Stay put, I’ll go and chase them away.” They giggled naughtily.

Bangani chomped in a big scoop of ice cream while Ithabeleng walked to the door. She was about to gobble down a second helping when she heard *his* voice.

“Oh, come on in. You have some explaining to do young man.” Ithabeleng let Letlotlo in, ready to fire him with questions.

When she turned and saw him. Handsome as ever. Bangani had mixed emotions. Fear, shock, happiness. She brusquely stood up from the couch. A little embarrassed, she squared her oversized t-shirt. It barely covered her short pants and she wished they could grow a few inches longer.

He looked at her. She was a mess. Messier than he had ever seen her. Yet she was still the prettiest girl he had ever laid his eyes on.

"Tlotla!" She exclaimed. "What a surprise!"

"Hey BK. Lovely surprise I hope?"

"*Aebo*! You disappear for weeks and you come here with your charm? Explain yourself *bhuti! O tswa kae?*" Ithabeleng grilled him.

Letlotlo was about to respond but Bangani gestured not to.

"*Mmata,* would you please be a darling and go help Roxanne to cash up? I'm afraid she could mess up my books and I don't have the energy to yell at her for her incompetence."

"Are you just going to chase..."

"Now, please *mmata*."

"I see what you're doing."

"Thank you, sweetheart. I love you!"

"Fine, *kea tsamaya.*" Sneering from Bangani to Letlotlo and back again, she added. "You kids must behave!"

"We promise." Letlotlo convinced.

Ithabeleng grabbed her car keys and waltzed out.

After the door banged shut, Letlotlo neared towards her just as she was also approaching him. They stopped half way from each other. A few inches apart.

"Firstly allow..." he expressed at the same time that she spoke out. "Tlotla, please..." They looked at each other and laughed.

"You first!" They echoed and broke into laughter again.

"God damn! You are beautiful." He exclaimed intently. She blushed. "I'm a mess."

"True, a beautiful mess."

"Stop lying."

"I mean it. How are you doing?"

"Under the circumstances? I'm surviving, thank you. How have you been?"

"Not so good. I missed you terribly." He confessed.

"You did? Is that why you called me to let me know of your whereabouts?" she asked sarcastically.

"Ouch! I guess I deserve that."

"Your mother blamed me for your departure. I blamed myself..."

"I left in such a hurry, BK. I was shocked by the revelation. I honestly did not plan on disappearing on you or my parents." He said.

"Do you have any idea how worried I was? I've beaten myself up, Tlotla. Why didn't you say anything?"

"I am so sorry. None of you are to blame. I just had to attend to an urgent personal matter."

"I wanted to be there for you."

"I know, sweetheart. Please forgive me."

"How could I stay angry at you? Come here, you foolish man." She smiled as they embraced in a deep longing hug.

"Daddy told me, but I want to hear it from you." He broke the hug and looked deeply into her eyes. Demanding assurance.

"That I love you? Are you that slow?" She nudged her elbow into his stomach and he laughed happily.

"Yes, I am that slow. Do you mind repeating it loudly so that I don't ever forget?"

"I love you, Tlotla."

"I love you more, Bangani Khumalo!"

"I missed you so much, Letlotlo Makhethe. I am deeply sorry for hurting you."

"Actually, it's Letlotlo Majara. And I missed you like crazy."

"Who?"

"Majara. Letlotlo Majara."

"Your surname? Wow. How come you never told me?"

"It was not relevant. The Makhethes are my parents. But you will be happy to know that I actually qualify."

"Qualify for what honey?"

"Your father's criteria."

"Oh, forget about that man. I love you regardless of who you are."

"It's good to hear that, my love. I am grateful that he had set the standards so high, I doubt I'd have found out my true roots if I was not so desperate to match his selection criteria."

"Hang on, are the Majaras like…"

"Yep, royal. One of the four regal houses in Lesotho." He guaranteed.

"Wow! Who would have thought?" She was amazed.

"God works in mysterious ways."

"That I believe! How did you find out?"

"I think we should sit for this one." He gestured.

"Of course. But let me make us coffee."

Letlotlo sat down while Bangani rushed to the kitchen and made coffee. She brought it on a tray with Danish cookies. He narrated the story from the last day they parted in devastation. What he prayed for when in isolation. The dream he had on his last day of the fast turned out to be God's way of answering his prayers about Zachariah's demands. He confessed that he left his parents and followed the messenger from his father's kingdom. The man he saw in his dream turned out to be his biological father, Morena Majara Selebalo. He was very ill and had tried everything to find the cure but nothing helped. Not medical experts nor traditional healers.

Doctors told Morena Majara that he needed a kidney transplant and that they had placed him on a long waiting list amongst others who needed donors. In dire straits, the messenger confessed that he and the family of the king's wife blackmailed Letlotlo's mother, forcing her to leave the country or they would kill her infant when they found out that she was pregnant by the then engaged king. They promised that they would take care of her and the baby if she protected the king's secret and stayed in hiding.

His mother kept her end of the deal and carried the secret to her grave when Letlotlo was still a toddler, giving him up to be adopted by the Makhethes. The King never knew that he had a son until when his life was in danger and the messenger confessed that there is a possible match.

According to Letlotlo, he was a match for the transplant but he did not donate his kidney. He prayed for his father and miraculously doctors could no longer detect the problem.

Bangani was amazed by this superior power. The one that qualified Letlotlo to be royal beyond a doubt. The one that healed his father when medical and traditional experts had failed. The same power that guided her to find her treasure (Letlotlo). She respected God more. She realised that indeed HE IS ROYAL!

EPILOGUE

Three years and a half later, Bangani was heavily pregnant with twins. They were staying in Butha-Buthe, Ha Majara in Lesotho, where her darling husband, Letlotlo Majara was the reigning King and branch overseer of BB Kingdom Fellowship Church. King Letlotlo Majara had ascended the throne in succession of his late father, Morena Selebalo who died peacefully in his sleep after kissing his first grandson by Letlotlo and Bangani. They named him Selebalo Majara Junior.

Bangani's Curio Shop was now a household name with different branches in major cities in several African countries. She was gratified that she was empowering women from underprivileged backgrounds to do beadwork and even promoted their other crafts in her shops.

Her rock pendant had won several awards at Art Festivals. Her proudest moment was when she spotted, in the Influential Woman Magazine, Dr. Auma Obama wearing the same pendant to the Africa Humanitarian Awards. They had interviewed Bangani and she shared her remarkable journey on how she got the inspiration to create that pendant.

While he was still conducting a council meeting, Morena Letlotlo Majara was bewildered when he was splashed with lots of water. When trying to retaliate, his right-hand man whispered that the action was a custom that confirmed that his wife had just given birth to bouncing beautiful daughters, *dikgametsi* (water bearers). He was overjoyed and uttered a silent prayer of thanksgiving. He was the luckiest man alive!

ABOUT THE AUTHOR

Lebohang Angelinah Mokhele is an author, scriptwriter, businesswoman and a servant in the house of God.

She confounded a church newspaper that published between 2015 and 2017.

She has written, co-directed and co-produced two short films in Sesotho, including the one where she captured the cover of this book working with raw talent (Sunday schoolers).

She has also produced, hosted a number of shows and anchored the news at a community radio station in QwaQwa where she currently lives with her family.

She was born and raised in Lesotho where she did all her formal education until obtaining a Bachelor's Degree in Animal Science cum laude with an award for Best Female Graduate in 2012.

Do not hesitate to reach out to her via social media on the following platforms

Instagram: @he_is_royal

Facebook: Lebohang Angelinah Mokhele and @he_is_royal

Cover designed by Lebohang Angelinah Mokhele

Cover models, Dumisane Radebe and Dikeledi Motaung
special cast of Mohlanka Wa Modimo (Servant of God)
Short film by Lebohang Angelinah Mokhele

www.ingramcontent.com/pod-product-compliance
Lightning Source LLC
Chambersburg PA
CBHW031318060726
47590CB00003B/1259

* 9 7 8 0 6 2 0 8 7 6 1 5 5 *